THE GIVING BAG BOOK

Give and you shall receive

Second Edition

Cara M. Hill

Halo
PUBLISHING
INTERNATIONAL

ISBN: 978-1-63765-110-0
LCCN: 2021916492

Registration Number: TXu 2-082-099
Date: 09-01-2018

Halo Publishing International, LLC
www.halopublishing.com

Printed and bound in the United States of America

This book is dedicated to my three wonderful children, Kamryn, Charlotte, and Bennett.

You inspire me to be my best self and I can only hope I do the same for you. I love you beyond words, you are all my biggest blessings.

It's Christmas time,
a time for giving, a time for
laughter, a time for family.

This is Grace, Ben,
and their parents.

Every year, Grace and Ben make their Christmas wish list.

And every year, their parents take them to see Santa.

Today's the day they get to go see Santa! Off they go with their lists in hand!

Grace and Ben
patiently wait to
sit on Santa's lap.

It's time. It's Grace and
Ben's turn to see Santa!

They walk up to Santa and sit on his lap.

"Yes, yes, Santa, we've been good, we've been kind to others, and we've listened to our parents!"

"That warms my heart," says Santa.

"What is that in your hand?" Santa asks. Grace and Ben take out their lists and begin to tell Santa what they wrote down.

After reviewing the lists,
Santa replies, "That is quite
a list! I will do my best."

Reaching behind his chair,
Santa pulls out a large bag
with a heart on it.

"This special bag is my 'Giving Bag.' You fill it with toys that you may not use anymore and clothes that you've outgrown. Once the bag is full, put it under your tree and once you are asleep, I'll send my elves to bring the bag back to the North Pole in a leap!" Santa explains.

Grace and Ben take the bag home
and fill it with forgotten toys and
clothes that are too small!

They put the bag
under their tree...

...and the next morning, it is gone!

They run to their parents' room
and declare the bag is gone; it's gone!

Their mom and dad came out to
discover that yes, the bag is gone!

"Now, doesn't that warm your heart that
you both gave up your things and children
who are less fortunate will now be able to
use them?!" says Mom.

Christmas morning finally comes.

Grace and Ben run down the stairs and they are amazed by what they see!

They sit down while their dad hands them presents with their names on them. Grace pauses and says, "Mom, Dad, because we gave our unused things away, that means other kids can have a wonderful Christmas like ours, right?"

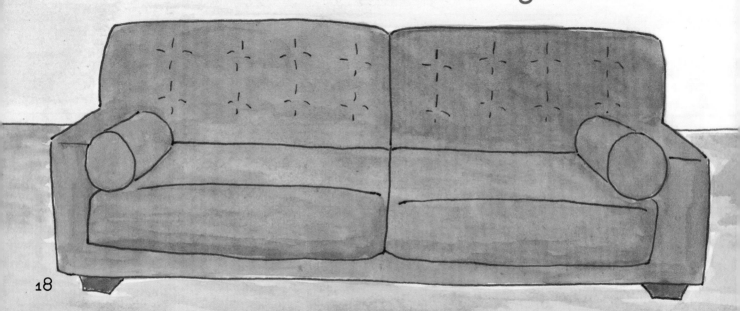

Dad responds, "Yes, Grace. Give and you shall receive. So, putting your things in the Giving Bag made other children have a wonderful Christmas too."

It is now your turn to fill up your bag
with unused or forgotten toys and clothes.

Here is a bag of your very own to fill
for Santa's workshop!

Parents, now you can discuss the following with your children to engage in conversation about giving.

What is giving?

Why should we give?

Who benefits when we give?